# A Very Merry Kissmas

## Samantha Baca

Cover Design: Richard Baca
Image (s): DepositPhotos

# Contents

# <u>One</u>
## Lucy

"Yes, Nana, I made it just fine. I'm at the cabin now."

I pressed my shoulder into the door as I held it open with my foot and struggled to free the key from the lock.

"I hate you being there all by yourself during Christmas," she said sadly.

"Don't worry about it. I'm fine, I promise. I wanted to be alone and spend it snowed in, somewhere in the middle of nowhere, with nothing to worry about and no pressing deadlines breathing down my neck. This is perfect. Thank you again for letting me come up here."

"Well, it's far from perfect." She sighed heavily on the other end. "I admit that I haven't taken care of it as well as I should have after your grandpa passed away. I'm getting too old to handle the things that I used to, and quite frankly, I have no idea how to do the things he took care of. I have someone who started doing some renovations, but unfortunately, there was too much to be done to have it ready before you got there."

"It has four walls and a fireplace. I think I'll manage just fine. I'm going to let you go so I can grab the groceries out of the car and unpack before it gets dark out." I spotted a coat hanging on the rack by the door, relieved to have something warmer to put on to go back outside. It was colder than I expected but surprisingly warm inside the cabin. Maybe I really was just frozen to the bone.

"Okay honey, enjoy your break and call me on Christmas if you can. I would love to at least hear your voice if I can't see your face."

"Will do, Nana. Love you."

"Love you too, sweetheart. Enjoy your night."

"You too," I answered as I pulled the other coat over what I already had on.

We hung up, and I grabbed the keys out of my pocket, ready to go grab my stuff when I suddenly heard running water. I stood still, tilting my head, trying to find where the noise was coming from. I knew there were a lot of things that needed to be renovated in the cabin, but she didn't say anything about a water leak. *That* was the last thing I needed to deal with right now.

I tiptoed down the hallway, scrunching my face as the wooden planks creaked beneath me.

I stopped outside of the bathroom, frowning when I found the door closed and steam billowing out underneath it.

*What in the hell was going on? Why hadn't I thought to go through the house and search it for intruders the second I came in? Probably because it's on the top of a mountain, and no one in their right mind would go out of their way to come up here just to hide in the shadows, waiting to murder someone when they finally showed up.*

I lifted my fist, ready to pound on the door and demand that whoever it was come out immediately, and then realized I didn't have anything to use as a weapon. I looked around and found a pool noodle that had been tossed into the spare room, likely from when my brother brought his wife and kids up over the summer to enjoy the lake at the bottom of the mountain.

I bent down, picked it up, and gripped it like a baseball bat.

I widened my feet, locked my knees, and swung a few times, ready to take on whoever was on the other side.

The sound of heavy metal drifted through the door seconds before it swung open, and I was startled by a gorgeous specimen wearing nothing but a towel around his toned waist.

"Freeze!" I yelled, raising my arms threateningly as the noodle flopped behind my head.

I narrowed my eyes and held my stance as he eyed me suspiciously, leaning casually against the doorframe. The towel started to shift and he made no effort to grab it. The outline of a one-eyed monster taunting me from beneath.

"Who are you, and what are you doing here?" I demanded, trying to make my soft voice sound intimidating.

"You must be Lucy," he answered, ignoring my question.

"How do you know my name?" I kept my eyes on him, trying to ignore the perfectly sculpted muscles that ran along his chest and abdomen, begging to be touched.

I did, however, take a few seconds to allow myself to check out the tattoos covering his skin—but that wasn't because I enjoyed them—it was a protective measure so I could give the information to the police and ID the intruder.

*He was 6'1, lean build with muscles protruding everywhere— and I mean everywhere. Dark gray eyes that hid beneath wild, wet hair that had fallen across his forehead until strong hands brushed it away. Well-groomed, with a thin goatee that dotted his jawline. A cross tattoo that covered his chest with a rose in the center and a woman's name written beneath it. A few smaller tattoos that covered his biceps and one on his thigh that I couldn't see all of because the towel was covering it. Stupid towel.*

He cleared his throat and pulled my attention back to him.

"You didn't answer my question—how do you know my name?"

"Your grandma told me you might stop by."

"Well, that's funny because she didn't mention anything to me."

"Is that supposed to be a weapon?" he asked, pointing to the pool noodle still being held in a death grip between my fingers.

"Maybe."

"What exactly were you planning to do with it? Whip me to death?"

He shifted his position slightly, but that didn't stop my eyes from immediately following the bulge beneath the towel, hoping for a glimpse.

"I don't have to explain myself to you," I said quietly, lowering the noodle to my side before tossing it back into the spare bedroom. "If anything, *you're* the one who needs to explain what *you're* doing here."

"Your grandma hired me to do some renovations."

She had mentioned that she had hired someone to get started on them but failed to mention that said person would still be here. Why hadn't she said anything and spared me an awkward surprise? I would have skipped the whole 'snowed in on a mountain' idea and booked myself a spa weekend at the Hilton instead.

"Okay, well, let me know when you're done, and I'll see you out."

"I'm actually done for the day. I was just getting ready to turn in for the night."

I shook my head, trying to clear the confusion so I could focus on what he was saying.

"So, what, do you like live close by or something?" I couldn't remember seeing any new houses that had been built since the last time I'd been up here.

"No," he paused as a grin spread across his devilishly handsome face. "I live here."

# A VERY MERRY KISSMAS

# Two
## Lucy

"Nana! You have some serious explaining to do!" I hissed into the phone, covering the mouthpiece as I hid in the bathroom.

"Did you see Dick?"

"NANA!"

How in the world was she being so nonchalant about this? It was one thing to know that he might still be up here when I got here, but it was another to just come out and ask me if I'd seen his wiener. Nana had always been a little cheeky, but even this was more direct than usual.

"What? Either you saw Dick, or you didn't. There's no need to scream about it."

I ran a hand over my face and tried to steady myself with deep breaths.

"No, Nana, I didn't see dick. He was wearing a towel, but it's not like he just whipped it off and gave me a show or anything," I said sarcastically, rolling my eyes that I was even having this conversation with her.

She burst into laughter on the other end, so loud that I had to pull my phone away from my ear because she was hurting it.

"Oh dear, sweet girl," she said with a chuckle. "His *name* is Dick. It's short for Richard."

My heart dropped in my chest as embarrassment washed over me.

"Oh. My. God. Why didn't you say something sooner?!"

"What was I supposed to say?"

"I don't know, maybe a heads up of—hey, there's this really sexy guy who's staying in the cabin doing renovations, and his name is Dick would have been helpful."

"I was sure he would be gone before you arrived. His mom said that she thought he was leaving this morning to come home for Christmas, so I figured it was pointless to tell you if he wasn't going to be there. I bet she will be disappointed that he won't make it after all. But I agree, he is quite handsome."

"Why won't he make it? I'm here now so he can leave and be on his way."

I ignored her comment about how attractive he was because I didn't need her getting any wild ideas in her head and trying to play matchmaker while I was up here.

"There's no way he would make it down the mountain now. The storm has already rolled in, so he's stuck up there until it passes."

"No," I countered in disbelief. "There has to be a way. What about the sled Grandpa used to have?"

"You're suggesting that he sled down the mountain in the middle of a blizzard?"

"I mean, it could be fun." I shrugged, judging myself in the mirror for being so petty right now. "I could give him a push just to make sure he got a good start."

"Lucy Nicole, you know better than that," she scolded. "I'm sorry that you have unexpected company, but I have to admit that it makes me feel a little better about you being up there by yourself this weekend. He really is such a wonderful man, kindhearted and caring."

"Then why did you offer to let me stay here if you were worried about me being by myself?"

"That was before I saw how bad the storm was going to get. I just caught the 5 o'clock news, and they said that Cedar Point is in for a real doozy. It's been building all day, but you were already on the road, and I didn't want to distract you while you were driving. I knew that if you could get to the cabin, you'd be fine."

"But you don't think I can take care of myself in a storm?"

"I think you can manage just fine, but you're a big city girl, Lucy. If the power goes out in the city, it's usually back on after a few hours. If you lose power in the cabin, it could be days or weeks before it comes back on again. Dick grew up here. He's used to the weather and knows how to improvise when needed. I know that he'll keep you safe and make sure that both of you have what you need to ride out the blizzard."

"Fine. I guess I don't have a choice since he's stuck here now. I can stay in the guest room since I'm guessing he's already claimed the master bedroom."

"Ummm," she hesitated. "About that."

"What?" Panic was spreading through me again. I hated the unexpected.

"There is no guestroom. After your brother stayed there this summer, we decided everything needed a major re-haul. Dick just discarded the rickety mattress and tossed the frame since the kids broke it while they were there. That thing was old and had seen better days."

I let my head fall forward and closed my eyes.

"Okay, so then, what are my options? Sleep on the couch? Use the recliner?"

"I wouldn't do that either," she laughed. "Nelly broke the springs in the couch while they were there. Your brother tried to fix it, but it was so old that he couldn't. I ordered new furniture last week, but it won't arrive until early January. Everyone is backed up right now, so we're at the mercy of when they can get it up the mountain and delivered."

"Lovely. Maybe this wasn't a good idea," I mumbled, instantly regretting my decision to come up here to *get away*. I'd left corporate hell in Phoenix to deal with small-town-stuck-on-a-mountain-with-a-stranger hell.

"I'm sorry, honey. I'm sure you'll find a way to make the best of it. But I've got to get going. Earl is dressed up as Santa at the senior center this year, and I'm next to sit on his lap and tell him what I want—if you know what I mean."

Before I could say anything, she hung up. I leaned against the door and counted to ten. Whether I was ready or not, I needed to face the sexy hunk that I would now be spending Christmas with.

# A VERY MERRY KISSMAS

# Three
## Rich

When my grandma warned me that Millie's granddaughter might come up to the cabin for Christmas, I wasn't sure what to expect. It had been years since my grandma had seen her, and all she could tell me was that Lucy was a fireball bigshot VP of a cosmetics company from Phoenix.

I had planned to get back down the mountain this morning, but a pipe burst in the bathroom, which required me to stay and deal with it. When I went into town to grab some supplies, I got one look at the clouds rolling in and knew I wouldn't be able to get out before the storm hit. I grabbed some necessities, making sure that I had plenty of food and water to get me through until I could get back to town again.

By the time Lucy came out of the bathroom, I was already dressed in a pair of gray sweatpants that hung low on my hips and a Cedar Point Bulldogs t-shirt. I wasn't huge on sports, but I wore their name proudly, given that my brother was their pitcher. They weren't too bad for a minor-league team that could fill the seats of every game.

When I walked in, Lucy was pacing the living room, looking for something.

"Everything alright?" I asked, trying to keep any hints of humor out of my voice, but it was hard with how adorable she looked.

Her straight brown hair was now piled on top of her head beneath a beanie, and her small frame was being eaten up by the oversized jacket she had on.

"Yeah. I need to go get stuff out of my car before it gets too late."

I glanced past her to the floor-to-ceiling window and arched an eyebrow. It was already pitch-black outside, and I could hear the wind howling as it whipped past.

"I think you missed that window about an hour ago. Tell me what you need, and I'll go get it."

"It's fine," she said, shaking her head. "You don't need to do that. I'll go."

She patted her pockets and then rolled her eyes, pulling a set of keys out.

"I would lose my head if it weren't attached," she murmured.

"My grandma would never forgive me if I allowed you to go out in this. Just give me the keys and tell me what you need."

"Don't worry, I won't tell. But I'm not going to have you run out in the storm to fetch my stuff. I'm a grown, independent woman and can get it myself."

"Would you stop being stubborn and just give me the keys?"

I sighed impatiently.

"You're not dressed to go out in that storm—you don't even have a jacket on."

"That's because you're wearing it."

She looked down and her face flushed with embarrassment again.

"Oh. I'm sorry. I saw it hanging by the door and just assumed…"

"That it was your grandma's? She's even shorter than you. She would trip over it." I laughed.

"No," she scoffed, narrowing her eyes at me. "I was going to say that I thought it was my brother's. And come to think of it, he's even bigger than you are. It probably wouldn't have fit him anyway."

I rubbed the back of my neck and shook my head, unsure what to do with her.

"While I would love to stand here and compare who is bigger, we don't have time for it. If I don't get the stuff from your car now, you're not getting it for a few days."

She scrunched her face and folded her arms over her chest.

"And why is that?"

"Because the snow is coming down faster than I can clear it. Give it another thirty minutes, and you won't even be able to find your car. Now give me the keys and tell me what you need."

She chewed her lower lip and then gave in, seeming to know she needed my help more than she wanted to admit. She shrugged off my jacket, gave me the keys, and followed me to the door to tell me what to grab and where it was.

# Four
## Lucy

Dick was right that the snow would completely devour my car, only it happened in twenty minutes, not thirty. I wondered why I didn't see his truck when I arrived, but he informed me that he had parked back by the shed. There was a clearing and the sun would melt the snow quicker once it came out again.

He grabbed the suitcases from the backseat and brought them to me before groaning when I told him there were boxes of stuff I needed from the trunk.

He moved quickly, and I tried to ignore the way he handled everything as if it weighed nothing. It took me almost an hour to get everything packed into my car before I left Phoenix and less than fifteen minutes for him to unpack all of it. To say that I was impressed was an understatement.

Once everything was inside, we stacked it in the living room since there was nowhere else to store it.

"How long were you planning on staying?" he asked, hanging his jacket on the coat rack behind the door as a smile snaked across his handsome face.

"I'm leaving the day after Christmas."

I grabbed a few of the food bags and headed to the kitchen to unpack.

"This is what you need for a *few days*?"

"Yes. This is what I need for a few days, and I didn't expect to have to justify myself to anyone, *Dick*."

I felt childish for mocking his name, but I was still on edge and nervous about the sudden change in plans that now included me being stuck here with a complete stranger. He watched me from across the island while I lined up the frozen meals that needed to go in the freezer.

"Can you please stop calling me Dick?"

I looked up and found dark gray eyes watching me.

"Why? That's your name, isn't it?" This time I was serious, and the mocking tone was completely gone from my voice. That was what Nana had called him, and she wouldn't lie to me or try to embarrass me by calling him that if it wasn't really his name.

"Technically, my name is Richard, but I go by Rich. Only my grandma and yours call me Dick. It's an old family name that my grandma insisted on keeping in the family when my mom had me."

"Oh, sorry. I didn't know. I won't call you that anymore."

"Thank you."

I lowered my head and avoided looking at him as I kept working.

"What's with all the frozen food?" he asked, nodding to the piles in front of me, effectively changing the topic for us.

I folded the tote bags and set them to the side before grabbing another one, desperate to keep myself busy so I could avoid looking at him.

"That's what I eat." I shrugged, not seeing what the problem was.

"You don't like real food?"

"It is real food," I countered. "It's just been preserved and frozen, so I can enjoy it whenever I want."

"You know as well as I do that those things don't taste nearly as good as a freshly cooked meal."

"Maybe. But some of us don't have the time to spend hours in the kitchen making meals for ourselves. I've been eating these for so long that I don't think about them anymore."

I hadn't realized until now just how long I had been in the mundane routine of getting home late every night and popping a frozen meal into the microwave, not even bothering to look at what it was first. When was the last time I had cooked? Better yet, when was the last time I'd sat down and enjoyed a freshly cooked meal?

He leaned against the counter behind him and studied me.

"You're a VP of a cosmetics company, right?"

"Yeah. How did you know?" I raised an eyebrow as I glanced up briefly while unpacking the last bag.

"Your grandma told me. She talks about you a lot."

I felt the heat prickle my cheeks as the embarrassment of what she might have been saying to him entered my mind. *Was she sitting around telling him embarrassing stories about me from when I was little? Had she told him about the time I lost control of the sled and hit a telephone pole straight on? Oh my GOD—had she shown him any of my baby photos?*

"Hopefully, all good things," I said, laughing nervously. "I feel bad that I don't call and check in with her as often as I'd like to."

The guilt started to eat at me the same way it always did anytime I thought about Nana. I was used to being busy and always on the go. It never bothered me because growing up, my parents were the same way. They both had busy, demanding jobs that required them to work long hours. My brother and I had spent a lot of time with my grandparents growing up, but once I finished high school, I was determined to get as far away from small-town Colorado as I could.

"I'm sure she understands," he said softly. "She's proud of you and everything you've accomplished. To be a VP by the time you're 25. Wow." He whistled through his teeth and tapped the counter with his knuckles before pushing off it.

"Thank you." I tucked my chin to my chest and avoided looking at him as I tried to absorb his compliments. I wasn't used to getting *this* kind of male attention, and my body reacted to it in a way that would leave me in an uncomfortable bind, given that there was only one bed, and we would both have to share it.

# Five
## Rich

The night went by faster than I had expected. I also hadn't expected to have company or to be figuring out how to share a full-sized bed with a beautiful stranger. When I met Millie up here a few weeks ago to talk about the demo work, she agreed that the beds in both the master and guest bedroom needed to be replaced. I'd taken the liberty of bringing over a blow-up mattress since I would be living here for a few months while I worked. It made more sense than driving an hour up and an hour back down the mountain every day to get to my home in Cedar Point.

"I can sleep on the floor," she said, looking nervously at the mattress as we stood in front of it.

"I don't think so. There's no way in hell that I'm letting you sleep on the floor. I'll sleep there if it makes you that uncomfortable to share the bed."

"I'm not going to let you sleep on the floor either," she scoffed. "I'm not kicking you out of your bed."

"Then it looks like we're sharing it." I placed my hands on my hips and smiled.

The wind was howling outside, so I knew it was only a matter of time before we lost power, which meant we would also lose heat. There was a fireplace in the living room, but tonight we would be more comfortable in the bedroom, where we could close the door and trap some of the heat in there until the morning.

"Okay, fine." She sighed heavily and looked around. "Which side do you want?"

"Take whichever one makes you more comfortable."

She eyed me for a moment before pointing to the right.

"I'm a side sleeper and sleep more on my left side. I'll take the right side so I don't startle you if you wake up and my face is next to yours."

"I think I'll be fine," I replied with a laugh.

"I wouldn't count on it," she said under her breath, climbing onto the mattress and pulling the blanket over her. She was smart and brought some thick sweats to sleep in, which would help fight off the cold once we lost power.

"Why do you say that?" I asked, waiting until she was settled before climbing in beside her.

"Because I'm an active mover in my sleep. I go to sleep in one spot and wake up in another. I also talk in my sleep when I'm stressed out, and sometimes, I get up and do things."

"Okay, maybe this was a bad idea," I teased, pulling the blankets back as I pretended to get out.

"You laugh now, but I'm serious. One time, I slapped my brother while he was in the sleeping bag beside me. It happened in this very cabin, out in the living room. He still gives me crap about it."

"What?" I laughed harder. "He still gives you shit over something you did as a kid?"

"No, it was last year." She winked at me over her shoulder before pulling the blankets under her chin. "Good night."

I laid down and shook my head, wondering what kind of night we had in store for us.

A few hours later, I was woken up by the sound of someone talking.

I rolled over and found Lucy twirling her hair around her finger while saying something to the wall across from her. Thankfully, she had warned me about talking in her sleep, otherwise, this might have freaked me out.

I couldn't remember what you were supposed to do with people who sleep talked or sleepwalked. I didn't want to startle her since she was still asleep, but she was also getting so loud that I couldn't sleep.

"Hey, Lucy," I said softly, trying to get her attention.

She didn't respond, simply just kept on with what she was doing.

I tried again, a little louder this time.

"Lucy, wake up."

Nothing.

I reached over and gently removed her finger from her hair and lowered her hand to her side. She curled it up into the blankets and shifted again. I thought for sure she was going back to sleep, but she just kept talking this time. Something about the tide going above the rocks, and if they didn't get out soon, the trolls were going to find them and eat them. Part of me wanted to stay up and listen to her stories because they were hilarious, but the other part of me was exhausted and needed sleep.

I gripped her shoulder and shook gently but with enough force to get her to turn over. Her eyes were open, but they didn't seem to focus on anything.

"Lucy?" I questioned, unsure of whether she was still asleep. It was dark in the room, so it was hard to tell for sure.

I shook her again, this time a little harder until she rolled over on her back. Her eyelashes fluttered as she blinked rapidly, trying to clear the sleep.

"What's wrong?" she whispered, looking around cautiously.

"Nothing, you were talking a lot, and it was getting louder, so I tried to wake you up."

"Oh, I'm sorry." She pulled her lips into a thin line and pulled the blankets up higher. "I told you I do that often when I'm stressed.

"I know, it's okay."

"If I do it again, just wake me up. I'll do my best not to, but I really can't control it."

"Okay."

We got situated, and she was back asleep before I knew it. It took me longer, but thankfully my body was tired enough to give in without much of a fight.

# <u>Six</u>
Lucy

I woke up the next morning tired and sore from sleeping on the air mattress. I missed my comfortable bed and the expensive pillows I had in Phoenix that helped wick the heat away from my head as I slept. I looked over and wasn't surprised to find Rich was already out of bed—if you could even call it that.

I stretched and got up, reminding myself I needed to take some time today for yoga and maybe a long, hot bath if the tub was still standing. I didn't look in the master bathroom last night to see what—if anything—had been done with renovations yet, but prayed that the large soaking tub my Nana had insisted on years before my grandpa died was still there.

The smell of coffee and bacon floated down the hallway, making me full on alert as my stomach growled. I had brought some granola bars and a handful of frozen breakfast sandwiches up with me, but I couldn't deny that the food Rich was cooking smelled heavenly.

I walked into the kitchen and cleared my throat, alerting him to my presence as he stood at the stove, flipping an egg in the pan.

"Good morning," I said, wringing my hands together anxiously in front of him.

"Morning."

He smiled over his shoulder before turning his attention back to the stove, but not before I caught a glimpse of a subtle bruise under his eye that wasn't there before.

"What happened to your eye?" I asked, walking over to get a better look.

He winced as he glanced at me, not letting me see it.

"Rich, what happened? Are you okay?"

"I'm fine," he insisted, transferring the fried egg to a plate. "Do you want eggs?"

I shook my head, trying to clear some of the morning fog still lingering around me.

"I have frozen breakfast sandwiches, but thank you. What happened to your eye?" I asked for what felt like the fortieth time.

He set the spatula down and turned to face me.

"You punched me in your sleep."

I gasped and covered my mouth with my hands.

"What? When? Oh my God, I am so sorry!"

"About an hour after I woke you up the first time. It's okay," he said, lifting his hands to keep me from reaching forward to touch it. "I'm fine. Really."

I stepped away, covering my face with my hands to hide my embarrassment.

"It's not fine. I can't believe I did that."

"It's not like it was on purpose. Was it?" His brows pulled together as he asked, his lips threatening to curl up into a smile at any minute.

"No," I laughed nervously. "It definitely wasn't on purpose. I am mortified."

"Don't be. It happens." He shrugged and cracked a few eggs into the pan before sprinkling salt and pepper over them.

"Does it, though? Because I can bet that if you polled 100 random people, you would be the only one who was accidentally punched in your sleep by a random girl sleeping beside you."

"Well, when you put it like that." He chuckled and gave me another delicious wink, his gray eyes inviting me to get lost in their depths.

I looked away, trying to spare myself from any further embarrassment.

"What can I do to make it up to you? Just say the word," I offered. The cabin was clean aside from where renovations were happening, so it wasn't like I could do much there, but I could try to help with something else. Anything else if it meant that I didn't continue to be eaten alive by the guilt that was consuming me.

"Have breakfast with me," he suggested, a flirty tone in his voice.

"Okay, sure. Let me grab one of my sandwiches, and I'll heat it real quick."

I went to open the freezer door beside me when he reached over and grabbed my arm, stopping me.

"What are you doing?"

"That's not breakfast. Have a *real* meal with me."

I chewed my lower lip, unsure how to answer him.

"I didn't bring anything other than the freezer stuff."

"So." He shrugged, flipping the eggs.

"I already took half your bed and beat you up while you slept. I don't want to take your food too."

He stopped and turned to face me again after moving the eggs to a plate and turning off the burner.

"You make it sound like I got attacked by some madman in the streets."

"Well…" I squinted my eyes and shrugged my shoulders. It wasn't a complete stretch of the truth.

"It's fine. I just need to know what you want. There's bacon, hash browns, and fried eggs. Tell me if you don't want something; otherwise, I'll fix you a plate."

"It all sounds delicious, thank you. Is there anything I can help with?"

He turned back to the stove and began serving the rest of the food onto plates.

"I've got it, thanks. I made a pot of coffee that you're welcome to, or there's juice in the fridge. Grab a drink, and breakfast will be ready in a minute."

I did as he asked and fixed myself a cup of coffee before joining him at the table in the kitchen. Everything smelled delicious, and I couldn't remember the last time that I stopped and sat down to enjoy a meal, and that thought made me sad.

We ate and made small talk, filling the awkward silence of two people forced to stay together who didn't know each other. Once we were done, I insisted on cleaning up since he'd done all the cooking. He went out to gather some wood from the screened-in porch, expecting that the power would go out soon.

It was surprising that it hadn't gone out already, but I was also thankful because I could use a nice, hot shower and didn't want to get stuck taking one in the dark. There was a small frosted window in the bathroom and a skylight that didn't bring in much light because of the thick tree branches that hung over it.

While Rich gathered the wood, I excused myself to go clean up. But really, it was just because I needed to get away from watching his toned body move the way it was every time he hauled wood in and tossed it into the bins beside the fireplace. He was strong and muscular in all the right places, with calloused hands that promised me a good time.

# A VERY MERRY KISSMAS

30

# <u>Seven</u>
## Rich

As expected, the power went out around two in the afternoon as the wind speed increased, and the snow fell in a blanket around us. We couldn't see anything outside through the windows; everything completely covered in white.

I had brought the last few loads of wood in before it really came down and set them in the living room corner while Lucy finished her shower. I didn't want to risk leaving them out on the porch, knowing that the snow would come in through the screen and get them all wet. Wet wood was the worst kind of wood unless a woman was involved.

I could hear the moment the power went out because she cursed loudly as if she had forgotten that I might be there. When she joined me in the living room wearing a Cedar Point Bulldog hoodie, I couldn't help but grin and wonder where she had gotten it and why she decided to bring it.

"What's with the grin?" she asked with a smile, pulling her legs under her as she sat in the oversized, worn-out recliner. "Did you hear me cussing in the shower and were worried that I was going to come attack you again?"

"No, I only worry about that when you're sleeping." I ran a hand smoothly across my face, trailing over the bruise she gave me. "Nice hoodie. Where did you get it?"

She pulled it away from her body and looked down as if she didn't remember what she was wearing.

"Oh, this? I got it from my Nana last year for Christmas. She goes on and on about the *best minor league baseball team of all time*." She used air quotes and an old lady voice to mimic her grandma. "Not only that, but I hear all about how the starting pitcher has the *cutest* little tooshie she's ever seen."

"I'll be sure to tell my brother," I said, my grin spreading wider as she gave me a curious glance.

"Why would your brother care?"

"Because it's his cute little tooshie she's talking about."

Her eyes bulged as she leaned forward and stared at me.

"Your brother is the starting pitcher for the Cedar Point Bulldogs?" she asked, gripping the armrests tightly.

"He's one of them. But definitely the most popular. Probably because he has the best butt. It runs in the family." I winked.

"Oh my God," she said with a giggle. "I can't believe my Nana is checking your brother out."

"Eh, he's used to it. All the women of Cedar Point do it. Hell, half of them have posters of him taped to their bedroom walls."

She scrunched her face and pretended to shiver.

I finished organizing the firewood in the built-ins next to the fireplace, admiring her grandpa for his design. It was beautiful and functional to have it off the floor and sitting right beside the fireplace so you could toss it in when needed. I also filled the extra baskets I'd found when looking for stuff in the shed the other day, just in case we ran low and required more before the storm passed.

"So, what do you do for the holiday?" I asked, looking over my shoulder as I finished up, noticing the way her eyes trailed over my ass.

*Was she checking me out?*

It wasn't the first time I thought she might have been, but the way she licked her lips as I leaned forward confirmed it.

I cleared my throat, startling her as her eyes quickly darted up and locked on mine.

I stood up, folded my arms, and watched her.

"I'm sorry, what?"

"I asked what you do for Christmas, but you were a little distracted, checking out my ass."

Her jaw dropped open as a flush of color kissed her cheeks. Her hair was pulled up into a messy bun on her head again, giving me the perfect view of it happening.

"What? I was not!"

"Hey, I know it's not as cute as my brother's, but I'd like to think it's still impressive. I do squats, you know."

"I swear, I wasn't checking you out," she whispered, her eyes widening again as I walked over and stood in front of her.

"Oh yeah? Then why are you blushing? It's because you got caught checking my ass out, and now you're trying to deny it." I lifted her chin with my finger, bringing her eyes up to mine. "Don't worry. I've been checking yours out, too."

# <u>Eight</u>
## Lucy

I couldn't believe that Rich had caught me checking out his ass. I was trying to be discreet, but I couldn't focus on anything other than how tight it was. Oh, and how I wanted to run my hands all over it before gripping it as he plowed into me. Not that he had offered or anything.

We sat in awkward silence for a few minutes until he got up and went outside for something, letting a rush of cold air in before he closed the door. I took a few minutes to gather myself and to try to quell the aching that was building between my thighs. Sure, it had been a dry spell of a few weeks, but that didn't mean I needed to jump his bones right now.

Okay, it was more than a few weeks. More like months. Twelve of them, to be exact. Twelve painfully dry months with nothing but my trusty vibrator to get me off when I needed it. Which, with the stress I faced constantly at work— was all the time. I was so impressed with its durability that I debated writing to Dark Vibes and complimenting them on such an incredible product. But how did one really write a raving review in an email about how much she loved their Dark Vibes G-Shocker without sounding a bit like a pervert?

I shifted in the recliner, trying to get comfortable, when I heard the door fling open, getting caught in a gust of wind. I turned around to find Rich stumbling in with boxes piled in his arms as he struggled to kick the door shut.

"Do you need some help?" I offered, getting up and rushing over.

"If you can get the door, that would be great."

He stepped out of the way while I pushed my weight into it, fighting against the wind until it finally closed and the lock latched into place.

"That wind is ridiculous," I muttered, following him into the living room, where he set the boxes down in front of the coffee table. "What's all that?"

"Well, I hope you don't mind, but I called your grandma and got the okay to bring the Christmas stuff out of the shed."

"You called my grandma?" I asked as my mind struggled to process the rest of his sentence. "What Christmas stuff?"

He bent down and lifted the lid to one of the boxes, revealing the decorations we used to put on the tree when I was a little girl. I covered my mouth with my hands when he lifted the angel tree topper and handed her to me.

It was always my favorite decoration, and I hadn't seen it in almost ten years. Once my grandpa got sick, we stopped coming to the cabin for Christmas and spent the holiday at their farmhouse in Cedar Point since it was too much on my grandparents to come up here.

"You didn't answer me earlier about what you do for

Christmas, but I could tell you seemed sad when I mentioned it. I came across these boxes a few weeks ago while cleaning the shed with your grandma. I thought maybe we could decorate since it is Christmas Eve." He shrugged and planted his hands on his hips while waiting for me to respond.

"I can't believe you did this," I whispered, clutching the angel to my chest.

His face fell, worry etched across his features.

"No," I assured him, crossing the room to where he stood. "This is amazing, thank you."

"Whew. I thought you were going to punch me again," he teased.

I shook my head and laughed.

"I'm not asleep. You're safe for now."

He winked and then began unpacking the artificial tree from the box while I sorted through the ornaments.

It felt like I had been transported back to my childhood, and memories washed over me in waves, pulling at my heartstrings and knotting them deep in my stomach. There were so many wonderful trips spent up here that I grew sad trying to remember the last time we had all been up here as a family.

The cabin was my grandpa's pride and joy. It was small and cozy, but he somehow worked magic to fit everyone in it when we all came up. It was always elaborately decorated on the inside and out, with warm lights creating the perfect ambiance to go with the apple cinnamon scent that was always softly permeating the air.

Once he got sick, everyone stopped coming up to the cabin, and I remembered how disappointed he looked. The fights he had with my grandma when he tried to reassure her he was fine and could make the trip up, even though we all knew how risky it was to get stuck up there without access to his medical supplies if he ran out.

Tears stung my eyes as I tried to blink them away. I had been so busy with work and starting my life that I hadn't even been there much for the end of his. I didn't come during the final trip when my brother brought my grandpa up for the day to hang out in the cabin while my grandma and mother packed up their belongings. I had tried to convince myself back then that it was fine and that they didn't need my help, but now I realized it wasn't that at all. I had avoided coming because I didn't want to deal with the pain I knew I would see on my grandpa's face as he said goodbye for the last time.

I clutched the angel to my chest and cried, not bothering to hold back the tears. Sadness enveloped me as I trembled, overwhelmed by the emotions racing through me.

"Hey," Rich said, pulling me into his arms and holding me tightly. "What's wrong?"

"I wasn't here," I cried, sobbing against his hoodie, still clutching the angel. "My grandpa died, and I wasn't here for him when he needed me to be."

"Shhh," he whispered, rubbing my back. "It's okay, Lucy."

We stayed like that for a few minutes as I fell apart in his arms, years of regret eating away at me.

# Nine
## Rich

"I'm sorry about earlier," Lucy said, barely peeking up to look at me as she continued to wrap the string of lights around the tree, handing the strand to me so I could continue on my side before passing it to her. It was getting late into the evening, so we were doing our best to work with what light we had from the candles and lanterns I'd set up earlier.

"Don't be. It's okay to feel whatever you're feeling. I'm sorry for bringing the stuff out without asking first."

"No, it's perfect. I didn't plan to decorate at all, but now that we have everything and we're actually doing it, it feels really nice. Kinda puts me in the holiday spirit, I guess."

"Good, I'm glad."

I took the last of the strand and wrapped it around the base, leaving the plug next to the outlet. We stepped back and took it all in, though I could imagine it would look even better once the power was on and we could see it lit up. It was still pretty with the decorations and made it feel a little more like the holiday.

"It's beautiful," Lucy whispered, wrapping her arms

around herself as she stared at it. "It brings back so many memories."

I smiled and then went back to the box, pulling out a bag of fake snow. I looked at Lucy, watching as she leaned over to see what it was. Her eyebrow immediately raised in warning as I tore it open and grabbed a handful.

"What are you doing with that?" she asked, stepping back.

"Decorating."

"That's going to make a mess," she warned, moving away as I advanced closer.

"I'm not afraid of a little mess."

She took another step back, this time bumping into the couch that needed to be hauled out and taken to the dump. I had her just where I wanted her.

Without warning, I brought my hand back and threw the fake snow at her like I would a real snowball if I had one.

Tiny bits of white plastic floated in the air around her, green eyes dancing wildly as they watched the pieces fall, coating her hair before they did.

"You didn't!" she exclaimed, staring at me in disbelief.

"Oh, I did. Whatcha gonna do about it?"

I grabbed another handful from the bag and tucked it under my arm before launching another attack on her. She moved quickly, careful not to trip over the coffee table before making her way over to the box and grabbing the other bag.

"It's on," she warned, ripping it open so hard that a cloud of white exploded in front of her.

"Is it? Because I think you should be more worried about me getting you again before you even have a chance to get your bag opened right."

I grabbed another handful and wound my arm up like I'd seen my brother do a million times during practice.

"You can run, but you can't hide," I warned, following her into the kitchen as she ducked down behind the island. I walked slowly, creeping up on her, when suddenly she whipped around it and came out of nowhere, smacking me upside the head with fake snow.

"You sure about that?" she teased, licking her lips. She reached into her bag and grabbed another handful, lifting it above my head before slowly releasing her fingers and allowing it to rain down over my head.

There was something in her eyes at that moment that made me forget all about the competition. I wanted to get lost in the depths of her green eyes and follow the light that had suddenly appeared, making her entire face look angelic.

We were standing close to each other, nearly toe to toe, our breathing heavy as we locked eyes and refused to look away. There was a powerful pull that I could tell she felt too, because her body kept leaning closer to mine.

"Fuck," I growled, pulling her into me as our mouths crashed down on each other.

She whimpered and deepened the kiss, her hands going up into my hair and gripping it tightly. I lifted her to my hips, grabbing her ass as she rubbed herself against my groin.

"Should we stop?" I asked, barely pulling my mouth away for a split second to talk.

"No," she panted, grinding harder against me. "I don't want to stop. I want this. I want it so bad."

I carried her down the hall to the bedroom and groaned when I remembered all we had was an air mattress. I felt like a college kid all over again, trying to get it on without even having a decent bed to offer her.

"I'm sorry," I muttered against her lips.

"For what?"

"Not having an actual bed."

"I don't need one. Now take off your pants."

"So demanding."

"If you only knew."

I lowered her from my waist, making sure she was good on her feet before I let go.

"Strip," I said, nodding to her as I pulled my hoodie over my head and tossed it to the floor. Her green eyes studied me intently, watching every move as I undid my buckle and worked the zipper down on my jeans, giving her a show.

"Now, Lucy," I growled, my voice snapping her out of her trance.

Her eyes snapped up to mine as my jeans fell to the floor before I stepped out of them. She slowly lifted her hoodie, bringing it up over her head, but taking forever. I crossed the space between us, wearing nothing but a t-shirt and boxer briefs that barely contained my erection.

I grabbed the hoodie and freed her of it before tossing it across the room. She stood before me, wearing a black lace bra and tight yoga pants.

"Fuck me," I whispered, thinking about all the things I wanted to do to her.

"I was kinda hoping you would," she teased with a giggle.

"How much do you like these pants?" I asked, slipping my fingers into the waistband and pulling her closer to me.

"They're my favorite."

"Then I suggest you take them off before I rip them off you," I warned, giving her a minute to do as I asked.

She moved quickly, keeping her eyes on me as she stripped down, showing off her bra and a matching thong.

I closed my eyes and bit my lip to keep from losing control and coming right then and there. I hadn't even touched her yet, and I was already losing it.

"You're so beautiful," I said, pulling her against my body again. My hands wandered over her smooth skin while my lips soaked up the taste of her skin, leaving goosebumps in their wake.

"Thank you," she replied softly, tipping her head back so I could kiss her neck while I rolled a pebbled nipple between my fingers through the thin lace of her bra.

"There are so many things that I want to do to you," I groaned. "But I don't think I can wait to be inside of you."

"I can't wait either."

I kissed her deeply, lifting her to my hips again as I walked us over to the dresser. I sat her on top of it, thankful that it wasn't too tall and looked sturdy enough for us to use. She spread her legs invitingly as I hooked my thumbs into the waistband of my boxer briefs and slid them down my legs. My erection sprung free, a drop of pre-cum glistening on top.

She licked her lips, watching as I stroked it slowly, teasing her as I stepped closer. I pinned her in as I reached to the side, grabbed my wallet from the top of the dresser, and retrieved a condom. I tried to steady my breathing as she leaned back on one hand and used the other to push her panties to the side, exposing her bare pussy to me. She licked her finger and then reached down and rubbed it down the middle of her slit, playing with herself as I locked every single movement into my memory and sheathed myself.

I stepped back slightly, mesmerized by how her features changed as she let her legs fall open wider, sliding a finger inside before pulling it out, coated with her wetness. She circled her clit, rubbing the moisture in a figure-eight pattern as her eyes pinched shut and her breathing grew rapid.

"Make yourself come," I urged, stroking my cock as she rubbed faster, already on the brink of an orgasm. "I want to see you come on your fingers."

She moaned and let her head fall back, holding herself up as her other hand came up and pulled the lace cup of her bra down. Her nipples were hard, begging to be sucked.

She rolled it between her fingers as her legs started to shake.

I wanted desperately to watch her as she fell apart, but I also couldn't keep myself from enjoying her tits that hung heavily above her stomach. I lowered my head and wrapped my lips around her nipple, sucking hard enough for her to hiss in response.

"Oh my gosh," she whimpered, rubbing herself faster. "I'm so close."

"Let me," I offered, letting go of my cock and pushing her hand away.

I replaced her finger with mine, my balls aching when I felt how fucking wet she was. I rubbed her in the same motion she had been rubbing herself, increasing the speed and pressure as her body reacted beneath me.

Within seconds, I felt the first spasm as her pussy locked against my finger, wrapping so tightly around it as she came. I continued to suck while I kept rubbing her clit, making sure she got every bit of that orgasm.

"Holy shit," she breathed, her dark lashes fluttering as she opened her eyes. "That was amazing."

I grinned and pulled my hand away long enough to grab my cock and line it up at her entrance.

"Good. Because we're just getting started."

# A VERY MERRY KISSMAS

# Ten
## Lucy

I tried to keep my eyes open so I could watch Rich's face as he plowed deep inside me, but it felt so good that I let my head fall back and just enjoyed every second. I couldn't remember the last time I'd been with someone, let alone the last time I had enjoyed sex. Usually, my mind was busy thinking about the laundry list of things I needed to do. Orgasms were never on those lists, given how infrequently they happened and how hard they were to come by.

I didn't date often, mainly because I never had the time, but when I did, I didn't bother waiting around to see if the guy knew how to get me off. I could usually tell within the first three minutes, and that was when they were usually finishing and pulling out with a condom filled with their release, not worrying about whether I had mine.

But Rich wasn't like that. There was something different about him, and that worried me. I was so quick to fall for his touch that I worried about what would happen if I never experienced this with anyone else. I knew that whatever this thing was that was happening between us was only temporary. A fling, for lack of a better word, and it would be over once I left and returned to Phoenix.

I could feel his butt cheeks clenching as he drove in deeper, my nails scratching his skin with need. His mouth lowered to find my nipple again, driving me wild. I could tell that he was getting close to coming, but instead of just pounding into me and getting off, he slowed his thrusts and began rubbing his thumb over my clit again.

"Come with me," he whispered, nipping my ear before returning his mouth to my other nipple. "Now."

I pinched my eyes shut harder, allowing my nails to dig deeper into his plump ass cheeks. I could feel the tease of another orgasm and desperately wanted it. He seemed to sense my frustration when I couldn't come easily this time and pulled his finger away.

I was about to tell him not to worry about it since I'd already had two, but before I could say anything, he pulled out and lowered himself between my legs. His tongue was hot against my sensitive flesh, lapping at the wetness before clamping down on my clit and sucking.

I almost bucked off the dresser, my nerve endings skyrocketing out of control as he continued his torture, bringing me even closer to climax.

"Oh, fuck!" I panted, reaching down to grab a handful of his hair.

He continued sucking, his tongue mercilessly working over me as I tightened around him seconds before allowing it to wash over and consume me. I knew he could feel it happening by his chuckle as I spasmed and clenched.

I cried out, my moans captured by his mouth as he crawled back up my body and sank inside me again. It didn't take long before he came, his body jerking violently with his release. Once he was done, he pulled out and helped me down as we tried to catch our breath.

"That was amazing," I breathed.

"It was," he agreed, still panting. "But next time, you come when I say so."

"Next time?" I questioned, laying down on the air mattress and smiling when he joined me.

"We're stuck here for a while until the storm passes. The power is out, and I don't know about you, but I think this is a fun way to pass the time."

I chewed my lower lip, trying to keep from giggling. He was right, and I couldn't say I minded having mind-blowing sex with a handsome stranger until the weather cleared.

"What about when we run out of condoms?" I asked, knowing that was highly likely, given that he was just staying up here to work on the renovations and probably didn't need a ton of condoms.

"We won't. Lucky for us, I stopped by Costco to stock up on supplies while I was in town. They happened to have a bulk box of condoms, so I grabbed them as a gag gift for my brother."

"Well, that's convenient, isn't it?" I teased, allowing him to pull me closer and wrap his body around mine. Cuddling with a gorgeous man in a room lit solely by candlelight wasn't a bad way to spend Christmas Eve.

# A VERY MERRY KISSMAS

# Eleven

## Rich

It was nothing short of a Christmas miracle to wake up with the power back on, given the storm that had rolled through. With the lights on, it gave me the perfect view of Lucy's amazing body as she slept sprawled out on the air mattress. The thin sheet barely covered her heavy breasts, the hardened nipples peeking over the top, begging to be sucked.

I felt my cock stiffen and shifted beside her to adjust myself. We had sex three times last night, and I still felt like I couldn't get enough of her. While I'd had my fair share of women, no one had ever come close to Lucy. She was a breath of fresh air, and I wanted to inhale and never let it out.

Last night was better than the night before in that she didn't assault me. She did roll over, and the next thing I knew, she was sitting on my cock, grinding over it until I woke up enough to put a condom on so she could fuck me. She wasn't sleeping, and I definitely wasn't going to complain about missing some sleep if it meant I got to be inside her.

Wanting to let her rest some more, I quietly rolled off the air mattress and went to the kitchen to start breakfast. Half an hour later, I heard her footsteps coming down the hall and felt a grin spreading across my cheeks.

"Good morning," I greeted, feeling her hand as it gently tickled my skin beneath the t-shirt I had thrown on. "The power is back on, so I'm making breakfast. Anything special you'd like?"

She leaned up and placed a kiss on my cheek.

"Good morning to you, too. Whatever you're making is fine with me. Can I help with anything?"

I turned my head and raised an eyebrow.

"Do you know how to make toast?"

She pulled her head back as if she were truly offended.

"It's toast! How hard can it be?"

I grinned and nodded to the counter where the toaster was tucked into the corner beside a fresh loaf of bread I had picked up at the store before the storm hit.

She worked on making toast while I finished up the omelets. They weren't anything fancy, but it sounded better than scrambled eggs. Part of me hated that it was Christmas morning and I didn't have a gift to give her. Then I had to remind myself that I hadn't planned to spend Christmas up here in the first place and that even if I had, I definitely hadn't expected to have company.

I flipped the omelet one last time before transferring it to a plate with sausage and hash browns. She brought a few slices of toast over a few minutes later and set them down while I cooked the next omelet. It was different cooking with her in the kitchen, especially with how little time we'd spent together. But it was fun to move around each other, grabbing what we needed and setting it on the table to enjoy another meal together.

When I turned to join her at the table, I stopped and felt my heart skip a beat to see it covered in a red tablecloth with some decorations we'd found in the box last night. There was a small vase filled with artificial poinsettias and two pine-scented green candles beside it. The table was beautiful, but it was dull compared to the girl sitting at it, shining like the brightest fucking star in the universe.

"Merry Christmas," she said cheerfully, extending her arms to show me what she had done.

"Merry Christmas. It looks beautiful."

*But not as beautiful as you.*

I wanted to spit out the constant compliments floating through my head, but I knew it would be better if I didn't. Lucy was only here for a few days, and then she would be heading back to Phoenix, back to a demanding job that would leave her little to no time for a relationship. Not that she had ever said she was interested in one, but I also wasn't the kind of guy who did the whole casual hookup thing aside from this.

It wasn't like I could expect this thing between us to work once she was gone. Lucy even admitted herself that she hadn't been back to Cedar Point in a while. Aside from a quick weekend trip with her brother and his family last year, it had been a few years since she'd been back. Why would I think that that would change for me? It wouldn't, and I needed to keep reminding myself of that.

"I didn't have a gift to give you, so I thought I could at least make it *feel* like Christmas," she explained when an awkward silence fell between us.

"I woke up feeling the same way," I said with a chuckle as I took my seat across from her. "Didn't have a gift for you either, and I don't think I've ever had a single Christmas where I've spent it with someone and didn't have something to give them."

"Me too. Though I usually stay in Phoenix for Christmas because work is insanely busy with holiday specials. My family and I mail our gifts to each other, and then I try to find time in the evening to FaceTime them so we can thank each other for the gifts."

"Isn't that lonely?" I asked, taking a bite of sausage.

She swallowed hard and looked down at her plate.

"Honestly? Yeah, I guess it is. I didn't realize how much I missed celebrating Christmas until last night when we decorated the tree together. It used to be my favorite holiday when I was a little girl."

"What changed?"

"Life." She shrugged. "My parents have always been workaholics, so it didn't faze me when we stopped spending the holidays together. I always knew that our family Christmas celebrations would stop once my grandpa passed. I guess I never realized how much I missed them until now."

"I'm sorry."

I wanted to reach across the table and hug the sadness until it lifted and the beautiful green returned to her eyes.

"It is what it is."

"Why don't you talk to your family and see if they want to start spending the holidays together again? I know your grandma would absolutely love it."

"It's not that easy," she sighed heavily. "My parents are so stuck in their ways that they won't change. My brother has his family, and they always have plans with his wife's side of the family, so it would be hard getting them together. I know my Nana is by herself, and I think the only thing that keeps me sane is knowing that she has her friends at the community center that keep her company. She always talks about how much fun she has there and how they do so much stuff for the holidays."

"She would leave all of that behind in a heartbeat if you told her you wanted to spend it with her," I said softly. "I know she misses the family holidays too, Lucy."

She studied her food, not bothering to eat it as she lowered her head and refused to look at me. I hated overstepping, but I felt she needed to know she wasn't the only one who missed it.

"A lot has changed since we lost my grandpa," she said sadly, her eyelashes lifting as she looked at me. "I thought I had to find a job that I loved and throw everything that I had at it, but I didn't even take the time to make sure that I *loved* this one before throwing everything I had at it. And do you know what the worst part is?"

She laughed, but I could tell it wasn't a happy one—it was the kind of laugh you have right before you lose your shit.

"What is the worst part?"

She leaned back in her chair and inhaled heavily before releasing it in one heavy breath.

"I fucking hate my job."

My eyebrows shot up, caught off guard by her statement.

"What?"

"It's true, I fucking hate my job," she laughed, covering her mouth.

"Then quit. Find something else."

"I can't do that."

"Why not?" I leaned back in the chair and wiped my mouth with a napkin. "If you hate your job, find something you love and quit."

"It's easier said than done. I have no idea what I even want to do. What I would be good at. I've spent so long working my way up the corporate ladder that I didn't bother to look around and make sure this was where I wanted to be. I make great money, but work my ass off and work so many hours that I don't have a life outside of work."

"Do you have any hobbies?" I asked, hoping that maybe that would give me some insight into what she liked to do so I could offer some ideas for new job opportunities.

"I haven't had time for anything in so long, I can't even remember. All I know is work, work, work."

"Well then, I guess it's a good thing you got stranded here."

"Why?" A grin pulled across her face, matching the mischievous one on mine. "What does that mean?"

"It means that you're in for a real treat because I'm buckets of fun." I gave her a playful wink as the wheels in my mind started spinning.

# A VERY MERRY KISSMAS

# Twelve
## Lucy

"You owe me big," I said, lifting the card to see how much.

"Ugh," he groaned, covering his face. "How much is it this time?"

"Well, with a hotel, you're looking at $1275. You'd think you would learn to stay away from Pacific Avenue, my friend."

He looked through his small stash of cash, both of us knowing he didn't have enough to pay what he owed for landing on my property.

"I'm a bit short," he said with a lopsided grin. "Would you, by chance, be willing to settle this with sexual favors?"

I ignored the spark that ignited between my thighs and shook my head no. I had been a total shark in this game, beating him three times in a row. It was like he was a glutton for punishment because he refused to back down and kept demanding a rematch. But that was probably because he was able to pay with sexual favors in the first match—not that I was complaining after my fourth orgasm.

"Fine," he sighed, looking over the board to see if he had anything else left to sell.

I grinned smugly, knowing that I had won another round.

"I can feel you watching me with those judgmental eyes," he teased, briefly glancing at me before returning his focus to the game.

"Hey, I'm just waiting for you to give up and admit you lost again."

"I let you win."

"Oh, really?" I arched an eyebrow and folded my arms over my chest.

"Yeah, you know, *anything* to cheer you up."

The dimple in his cheek was even more prominent the deeper his grin spread as he leaped across the floor and tackled me, tickling my sides as I struggled to contain my laughter.

"That's cheating!" I squealed, loving the way his body felt on top of mine.

"No way." He dug his fingers into my side, pressing harder against me as I laughed and struggled to get free. "The only cheater in this room is the one who won four games of Monopoly in a row. There's no way you're just that good."

"What can I say?" I said breathlessly, giving in and allowing him to pin my arms over my head as he laid on me. "I've always loved the game. I've been the reigning champion in my family since I was seven."

"Really?"

I nodded and felt my body start to relax again.

"I've always loved real estate, and playing Monopoly was always intriguing because I loved its strategy. I think that taught me a lot about what I needed to know in my current job. It's the same strategies I find myself using at work, and that's the only thing I love about my job."

He rolled off me and sat up, giving me a puzzled look.

"Why don't you do that?"

"Do what?" I frowned, sitting up beside him.

"Why don't you quit your job and go into real estate instead?"

"Ha!" I snorted. "There's no way I can just quit my job and move into a different field. Plus, I would have to study and pass an exam to be a licensed realtor. Where would I find the time to do that?"

"You'd have plenty of time if you quit," he said with a shrug of his shoulder.

"Okay, but how am I supposed to pay my bills without a job? I know I beat you four times in Monopoly, but even you have to admit that it wouldn't be a sound financial decision to give up a steady stream of income for something unknown. Phoenix is brutal; there's no way I could afford to live there without the income I currently have."

He nodded, but I could tell there was something he wanted to say but wouldn't.

"I appreciate the suggestion, really. It's just not as easy to make that big of a change. My life is too busy, too complicated."

"And you hate it," he blurted out.

I pulled my head back, slightly offended.

"I'm sorry, but you do. You've admitted it yourself."

"I said there were things I didn't like about it, but I never said that I *hated* it."

"You said you hate your job," he said sharply. "And that you missed spending the holidays with your family. Come on, Lucy, is there anything you actually love about your life? You don't have to lie to me, and you definitely shouldn't keep lying to yourself."

I paused momentarily and thought about it, frustration mounting when I couldn't think of a single thing I loved about my life right now.

"No," I sighed, hating the way I felt right now. "There's nothing I love about it."

He leaned forward and held my chin between his fingers.

"Then why not start over and make it something you love?"

"How?" I asked, not pulling away from his touch.

"Move back to Cedar Point. Live with your grandma for a bit or stay up here with me. You know as well as I do that things aren't as expensive up here, and your grandma isn't going to let you pay rent regardless of who you stay with. You can find your happiness again, Lucy. You just have to try."

# Thirteen
## Rich

Lucy didn't say much after I asked her to move back to Cedar Point. I couldn't blame her, though, given that I'd sprung the idea on her and asked her to move in with me to a house I didn't even own.

*What the hell was wrong with me?*

She was what was wrong with me. She'd gotten under my skin in a matter of days, and now I couldn't imagine not having her with me. I wanted to spend every day with her, watching her laugh and every night making love to her.

By lunchtime, we'd both sat down to eat, though we didn't say much other than some small talk about the storm outside. The power had stayed on for a while, so I felt confident that it wouldn't go out again. That also meant that the worst part of the storm was over, and Lucy would be able to leave and go back to Phoenix sooner than I wanted her to.

Needing some space to clear my head, I went and took a long, hot shower after cleaning up the mess from lunch. When I went back to the living room, I found Lucy on the floor in front of the entertainment center, searching for something in one of the cabinets.

"What are you doing?" I asked, sitting on the arm of the couch so I didn't crowd her.

"Looking for something," she said quietly, picking up an old photo album and looking at the cover before putting it back. "There it is!" She got up and took it to the kitchen table, inviting me to join her.

"This was the first Christmas up here that I remember. I was five and so disappointed that Santa wouldn't come to our house if we weren't there. My parents tried desperately to convince me otherwise, but I wouldn't listen and was in a complete meltdown when we arrived. My grandpa pulled me up onto his knee and asked what was wrong. When I explained it to him, he simply nodded and said he understood.

"We sat down for dinner, and I thought it was odd how quickly he ate before he excused himself from the table. Once we were done cleaning up, we sat in the living room, watching a movie on the TV while keeping warm by the fire. Suddenly, there was a heavy thud outside and then a loud knock on the door. When my dad opened it, Santa was there with a heavy bag filled with presents."

My cheeks split as I listened to the story, knowing exactly where she was going with the story.

"I waited my turn and sat on Santa's lap, doubting that he was the real thing. When I told him that, he tipped his head back and laughed. I told him that Santa was supposed to come down the chimney, not the front door. Do you know what he said to that?"

"What?"

"You're the one who lit the fire. I wasn't going to burn my ass off to get these gifts to you!"

We both burst into laughter, Lucy blotting the corners of her eyes as tears formed.

"My grandma scolded him, then realized she was about to blow his cover and stopped. I hadn't noticed that it was him because I was so stunned that Santa had said *ass*."

"That was nice of him to do that for you."

"He was the nicest guy I've ever known. He'd give the shirt off his back to someone if they needed it."

"Was he already planning to dress up as Santa?"

"No," she laughed even harder. "No one had even given it any thought because my parents usually took us to the mall on Christmas Eve to see Santa before he left to deliver gifts. Since we didn't go to the mall, they completely forgot about it. My grandpa used to dress up as the Santa down in Cedar Point, so he already had a suit."

"Where did he get the gifts from then?"

"That's the hilarious part," she giggled. "He took them from the stash my grandma had hidden for Christmas morning. She chewed him out for messing up her piles and not asking beforehand."

"Sounds like it was a fun time, though."

"It really was. That was when my parents seemed happy and weren't constantly on their phones, checking in for work. Most of my memories of Christmases after that are of my grandparents and brother. I know my parents were there, but I don't remember much about them being there."

"I'm sorry. That sucks."

She shrugged and flipped the page, smiling as memories came through with the pictures.

"I used to love coming up here."

Her voice had so much sadness that it pulled at my heart and made it ache for her.

"Life was so much easier, and I used to tell myself it was because it was a vacation. Life is always better when you're on vacation and not stuck in the daily rut you need a break from. But part of me wonders if life really is just easier up here. Away from the masses of people. The chaos. The unfulfilled void that lingers around you."

I shifted in the seat beside her, folding my hands in front of me as I tried to figure out how to say what I wanted.

"I love my life in Cedar Point. It's calm and predictable, but that's what I love about it. I take breaks and go fishing at the lake during the summer, or sometimes I take a few days to go skiing in the winter. But other than that, there's nothing else that I crave or feel like I'm missing."

*Other than you now that I've met you.*

"That must be nice," she teased, bumping her elbow with mine.

"It is. And I wasn't lying when I said that you could have all of that too. Move back to Cedar Point, Lucy. Start over and give yourself a second chance. Give *us* a chance."

Her fingers trembled as I reached over and covered her hand with mine.

"That's a lot to ask for, Rich."

My stomach sank, along with my hopes and dreams of having her with me.

# A VERY MERRY KISSMAS

# Fourteen
## Lucy

Things felt off and strained between Rich and me after I declined his invitation to stay with him. It wasn't that I didn't want to say yes and jump on the opportunity of a lifetime. I was scared, and I didn't want him to see me fail if things didn't work out how I needed them to.

We kept our distance for a few days while I stayed stuck on my phone, dealing with emails and taking calls while I worked remotely. The roads were still being cleared, so I had to wait for them to get all the way to the top of the mountain. But my work didn't care about any of that since my holiday vacation was technically over on their end. Every night I was drained from the overwhelming amount of things piled up on my plate, and I hated that I had become the same grumpy person I was back in Arizona.

Rich was nice enough to give me space and keep his distance while he worked on some of the renovations. We both kept an eye on the weather—me so I could leave and get back to Phoenix, and him so he could leave and celebrate the missed holiday with his family.

I tried not to dwell on the fact that mine hadn't even seemed to realize that they'd missed talking to me on Christmas. Aside from Nana, no one even texted to wish me a Merry Christmas. I FaceTimed her as she'd asked, and she was pleasantly surprised to see Rich and me together as we both wished her a Merry Christmas.

Something pulled tightly in my chest, making me miss the holidays I'd spent at the cabin when I was little. Looking through the photo albums had been wonderful, but they did nothing to replace the emptiness I felt when I thought about returning to Phoenix.

I sat in the recliner, responding to another email that had just come in and was marked urgent. It was after ten o'clock and I should have turned my phone off hours ago. My fingers flew across the keypad, typing a response as a call interrupted me.

"Hello, Jacinda," I said, trying to keep the annoyance out of my tone as I greeted the president of Clutch Cosmetics.

"Lucy, yes, there is an urgent matter that requires your immediate attention. I've sent an email and outlined the portions of the upcoming—"

"It's ten o'clock at night," I blurted out, interrupting her. The tone in my voice grabbed Rich's attention as he put his tape measure away and watched me.

"I'm well aware of the time," she snapped. "But pressing matters call for attention. As the VP, it is your responsibility to—"

"No," I said firmly, standing up and taking a deep breath. "I quit."

I heard a low gasp on the other end.

"Excuse me?"

"I said I quit, Jacinda. You heard me. I quit. I quit you. I quit Clutch Cosmetics. I quit everything."

"You can't just quit," she scoffed. "You need to provide a two-week notice, and you can start that by responding to the email I—"

"No," I interrupted again. "I will not respond to anything. Arizona is an at-will employment state, meaning I have no obligation to provide any notice of my resignation. Which, by the way, is effective immediately."

My fingers trembled as I struggled to hold on to the phone.

"I'm sorry. Let's take a step back and calm down before we make any rash decisions."

"I'm good with my decision. It's final. I'll be in to collect my things in a few weeks once the roads have cleared and I can safely make it back to Phoenix. Until then, do not call, text, or email me unless it's regarding my unpaid PTO and final check. I'll copy you on the email I send to HR, confirming my resignation and the hours of leave I'm entitled to take."

Before she could object, I hung up the phone and tossed it into the chair behind me. Rich rushed over, studying my face as he cupped it in his hands.

"Are you okay?" he asked.

I covered my mouth with trembling fingers.

"I don't know what happened," I laughed nervously. "I've

never quit a job before, but she made me so mad. I just snapped."

"I don't blame you. Enough is enough."

"What am I going to do now?" I could feel the panic coursing through me as I refrained from picking up my phone and calling her to beg for my job back.

"Move in here with me. Take some time to get on your feet again, and then decide what you want to do from there."

"I can't just move in with you," I said with a laugh.

"Why not?"

"Because it's crazy! We don't even know each other, and what if we get tired of being around each other? Plus, I need a real bed soon—no offense."

"None taken. And a *real bed* is being delivered as soon as the rest of the road clears. I got an email from the delivery company tonight, and they think they can get the beds for the guest room and the master bedroom here in two to three days. If you can handle the air mattress for a little longer…"

I worried my lip between my teeth while I considered it. Everything in my life had always been so rigid and perfectly regimented that it felt weird to be so reckless and liberated. But maybe that was *exactly* what I needed. Maybe that was the thing that was holding me back from the happiness I was desperately searching for.

"Okay," I sighed, giving him my biggest smile. "But before we commit to anything, I do have one question to ask you."

"Sure. What is it?"

"Since your name is Richard but your nickname is Dick, does that mean if you take a dick pic, it's really a selfie?"

I tried to keep my face straight to keep the laughter from bursting out of me.

His cheeks split into the most beautiful smile I had ever seen before his head tipped back in laughter. He leaned down and pulled me up from my seat, tickling my sides as he wrapped his arms around me.

"You think you're cute, don't you?" he teased, his mouth nipping at my ear.

"The cutest."

"Indeed." He stepped back for a second and studied my face. "You sure you want to do this?"

"Yes," I replied confidently. "Let's do this!"

# Epilogue
## Lucy
## Six Months Later

"Do we have everything ready?" I asked, rechecking the tote bags.

"Yes. We have everything we need, and if we don't, I can drive back up to get stuff."

"Okay. Sorry, I'm just nervous."

"Don't be. It's going to be fun, you'll see."

I took a deep breath and slowly released it, trying to remind myself that planning a family reunion wasn't a terrible idea.

Instead of having everyone come stay up at the cabin like we used to do, I rented out a few of the cottages that Rich and I were currently managing. It turned out that it wasn't real estate that I loved as much as it was property management.

Shortly after I quit my job as VP of Clutch Cosmetics, Rich went with me to Phoenix to collect my things and terminate the lease on my apartment. It was exhilarating and freeing to walk away from everything, knowing that I was heading down a path that had already made me happy.

I moved in with Rich and helped him with the cabin renovations, surprised by how much I enjoyed the physical side of it. Not only that, but I had a great view of watching him work as well.

Things had been running smoothly, and once the cabin was done, Nana came up to check it out, handing me the keys to my very first house. Rich was renting his house in Cedar Point to a new family in town, which felt like another piece of the puzzle falling into place.

We packed the Jeep full and then headed down to meet everyone at the lake. I'd invited my family, and Rich invited his. It was fun and exciting but also super nerve-wracking, given that I had never met the parents of anyone I was dating, nor had my family ever met any of the guys I dated.

When we pulled up, my brother's truck was already there, and his wife was busy setting up the food under the pop-up tent with Rich's parents. He had a pile of rafts he was working on blowing up while the kids took the time to lather themselves with sunscreen. We were a few minutes late, but I was thankful that everyone had apparently taken the time to introduce themselves, and there didn't seem to be any awkwardness about it. I glanced around, not spotting my parents, even though they had assured me they would be there.

We parked and got out, the humid air wrapping around us. I helped Rich unpack the food stuff before taking it over to the tent while he handled the rest. The energy around us was fun and exciting as everyone prepared for a day at the lake. I loved these trips when I was little, and I had hoped that I could recreate that feeling by calling everyone together for a family reunion.

Nana came over with Rich's grandma, the two constantly looking like they were up to no good. They made it a point to brag about how they succeeded in setting us up and joked that they should start a Cedar Point dating service. They joined us for a few minutes making small talk before heading over to see what kind of trouble the kids were getting into. I opened a bottle of water and took a sip, nearly choking when I spotted my parents' Lexus pull up.

The doors opened, and my mom got out, lifting her hand to shield her eyes as she looked around before spotting me. She gave me a quick wave before pulling her sundress over her head and tossing it into the car.

My dad came around, and I burst into laughter when I spotted the swimsuits they were wearing as they walked toward us, holding hands.

When I sent out the invites to the reunion, I'd included one of my favorite family photos that had been taken at this very lake almost twenty years ago. In the picture, my mom wore a one-piece swimsuit with a giant pineapple stretched across the front, while my dad wore neon pink swim trunks.

It was as if we were reliving that moment as they paraded over, showing off the lookalike swimsuits from the photo.

"Oh, my gosh!" I squealed, pulling them both in for a hug. "Where did you guys find these?"

"Amazon," my mom replied with a laugh. "It turns out you can find almost anything on there."

"I'm so glad you guys could make it. Thank you for coming."

We hadn't talked much about me quitting my job,

mainly because I felt like they must have thought I was a disappointment for not being as dedicated to work as they were. Maybe that was why I felt the need to include Rich's family today, sort of a buffer to keep the attention off of me that I didn't want right now. I just wanted to get back to spending time with my family.

"Thank you for putting this together. Sometimes, it's nice to take a step back and remember where you came from." My mom squeezed my hands while my dad took off running to the dock that everyone loved jumping into the lake from.

"Cannonball!" he yelled before diving in.

"Just like old times," my mom said wistfully before walking around and saying hi to the rest of the family and introducing herself to Rich's.

I stood there grinning like a fool when Rich came up and wrapped his arms around me. I tilted my head to the side to give him access as he planted kisses down my neck.

"You better knock it off, Dick," Nana warned, shaking her finger. "This here is a family establishment, and we won't be having no hankey-pankey business going on."

She turned and pointed her finger at my mom, who shrugged and then winked at us. Nana and Rich's grandma linked arms and snickered like school girls before walking off to grab a beer from the ice chest.

"Be thankful for that, or you wouldn't be here." My mom winked, and I heard a low chuckle deep in Rich's throat behind me.

I felt my cheeks burn as I blushed. My mom turned away, giving us a moment to ourselves.

I lifted my head back and leaned into him.

"Tell me again how you get Dick out of Richard?"

"You ask nicely," he growled, nipping my ear.

"Or maybe I could just tell you how much I love you and that even though your brother may be known as the pitcher with the cutest ass, I still think yours is ten times better."

"I love you too." He leaned in and gently kissed the tip of my nose.

"My ass is *the best,* and people literally spend money to come see it in action," his brother teased as he passed by, eavesdropping at the perfect time, given that I hadn't seen him walk up on us. He grabbed a beer and headed to the dock to join everyone else.

"People would pay to see mine if I asked," Rich called out, earning a middle finger in the air from his brother as he kept walking and didn't look back.

"And if anyone has the best ass—it's you. Now let's leave so I can take you home and ravish it." He wiggled his eyebrows playfully.

I giggled as his fingers tickled my sides, making everything inside me feel alive again. I thought I had everything I wanted out of life until I met Rich and he taught me how to live again.

*******************

Looking for more steamy holiday novellas? Be sure to check these out!

### **<u>Sugarplum Falls Series:</u>**

Blame It On The Mistletoe

https://books2read.com/u/bw1rqe

Blame It On The Eggnog

https://books2read.com/u/38PPY6

Blame It On The Candy Canes

https://books2read.com/u/31DNo7

Blame It On The Blizzard

https://books2read.com/u/b6z6XE

### **<u>Standalones:</u>**

Snow Place To Go

https://books2read.com/u/4A560N

A Christmas Wish

https://books2read.com/u/4EKXpE

Holiday Hijinks

https://books2read.com/u/4DP6Ze

# Other Books By Samantha Baca

## **The Haven Brook Series**
## **(small-town romantic suspense):**

'Til Death Do Us Part (Haven Brook Book 1)

https://books2read.com/u/m2RJNR

The Cradle Will Fall (Haven Brook Book 2)

https://books2read.com/u/b6O0QE

The Ties That Bind (Haven Brook Book 3)

https://books2read.com/u/mqgoz8

A Very Haven Christmas (Haven Brook Book 4- Novella)

https://books2read.com/u/mvqGjj

Three Strikes, You're Gone (Haven Brook Book 5)

https://books2read.com/u/mvqL2z

## **<u>The Dark Shadows Trilogy</u>**
## **<u>(romantic suspense)</u>**

Five Steps Ahead (Dark Shadows Book 1)

https://books2read.com/u/38Q0gO

Ten Seconds Too Late (Dark Shadows Book 2)

https://books2read.com/u/3JRgVB

Against The Clock (Dark Shadows Book 3)

https://books2read.com/u/m2YwoR


## **<u>The Stone Creek Series</u>**
## **<u>(small-town- novellas)</u>**

Chocolate Covered Mistletoe (Stone Creek Book 1)

https://books2read.com/u/3LRk9N

Candy Coated Promises (Stone Creek Book 2)

https://books2read.com/u/mldP5Y

Pumpkin Spiced Possibilities (Stone Creek Book 3)

https://books2read.com/u/bojdwV

# **Beaumont Creek Series**
# **(small town)**

Just One Time (Beaumont Creek Book 1)

https://books2read.com/u/3G52zK

Second Chances (Beaumont Creek Book 2)

https://books2read.com/u/4Aj6Z0

Third Time's The Charm (Beaumont Creek Book 3)

https://books2read.com/u/b5lEyG

Four-ever Single (Beaumont Creek Book 4)

https://books2read.com/u/4j5jMX

Fifth Wheel (Beaumont Creek Book 5)

https://books2read.com/u/4XwKwa

## **<u>Whiskey Mountain Series</u>**
## **<u>(small-town- novellas)</u>**

Something To Talk About

https://books2read.com/u/4X62ag

Something To Think About

https://books2read.com/u/3GWAan

Something To Believe In

https://books2read.com/u/3yVzgB

Something To Live For

*Preorder link coming soon*


## **<u>Sugarplum Falls Series</u>**
## **<u>(Holiday Novellas- can be read as standalone)</u>**

Blame It On The Mistletoe

https://books2read.com/u/bw1rqe

Blame It On The Eggnog

https://books2read.com/u/38PPY6

Blame It On The Candy Canes (coming 11/3/23)

https://books2read.com/u/31DNo7

Blame It On The Blizzard (coming 11/17/23)

https://books2read.com/u/b6z6XE

## **<u>Standalone Books</u>**

One Last Wish

<u>https://books2read.com/u/mqg7D9</u>

Finding Love In Apartment 2C (novella)

<u>https://books2read.com/u/bze9aZ</u>

Cocky Counsel: A Hero Club Novel

<u>https://books2read.com/u/31Kzkn</u>

All Is Fair In Food And War (novella)

<u>https://books2read.com/u/bp8qjX</u>


## **<u>Holiday Books (novellas)</u>**

Snow Place To Go

<u>https://books2read.com/u/4A560N</u>

A Christmas Wish

<u>https://books2read.com/u/4EKXpE</u>

Holiday Hijinks

<u>https://books2read.com/u/4DP6Ze</u>

# About the Author

Samantha lives in the southwest with her husband and two small children after abandoning her childhood dream of living in a cabin in Colorado when she found that she couldn't afford to live there and was deathly allergic to the woods. When she's not writing, she's usually spouting off sarcastic remarks while drinking wine out of a coffee mug to look like a functional adult while chasing down her toddlers. She enjoys spending time with her family, watching reruns of Friends, and the 24/7 flow of coffee that can be found in her veins. Be sure to follow her on social media for updates on what she's working on.

You can find her here:

Facebook: https://www.facebook.com/AuthorSamanthaBaca

Instagram: https://instagram.com/author_samantha_baca

Goodreads: http://www.goodreads.com/authorsamanthabaca

Facebook Reader Group:https://www.facebook.com/groups/2945710968775398/

Webpage: https://authorsamanthabaca.wordpress.com

Newsletter: http://eepurl.com/g0NcSj